Quentin Blake

MISTER
MAGNOLIA

MISTER MAGNOLIA
A RED FOX BOOK 978 0 099 47565 1

First published in Great Britain by Jonathan Cape,
an imprint of Random House Children's Books
A Random House Group Company

Jonathan Cape edition published 1980
Red Fox edition published 1999
This Red Fox edition published 2008

7 9 10 8 6

Red Fox books are published by Random House Children's Books,
61–63 Uxbridge Road, London W5 5SA

www.kidsatrandomhouse.co.uk
www.rbooks.co.uk

Addresses for companies within The Random House Group Limited can
be found at: www.randomhouse.co.uk/offices.htm

THE RANDOM HOUSE GROUP Limited Reg. No. 954009

A CIP catalogue record for this book is available from the British Library.

Printed in China

Mr Magnolia has only one boot.

He has an old trumpet

that goes rooty-toot –

And two lovely sisters
who play on the flute –

But Mr Magnolia has only one boot.

In his pond live a frog
and a toad and a newt –

He has green parakeets

who pick holes in his suit –

And some very fat owls
   who are learning to hoot –
But Mr Magnolia
   has only one boot.

He gives rides to his friends

when he goes for a scoot –

And the splash is immense
when he comes down
the chute –

But Mr Magnolia
has only one boot.

Just look at the way that
he juggles with fruit!

The mice all march past
as he takes the salute!

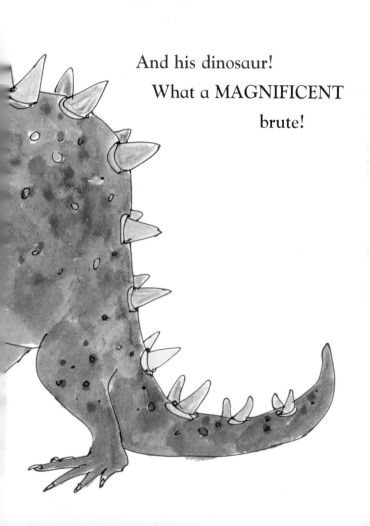

And his dinosaur!
What a MAGNIFICENT
brute!

But Mr Magnolia –
    poor Mr Magnolia!
    – Mr Magnolia
        has
    only one boot . . .

                Hey –

Wait a minute . . .

Now then . . .

Keep going . . .

What's this?

Look!

It's a boot!

It's a boot!

Whoopee
for Mr Magnolia's
new boot!

Good night.